Dear Parents:

Congratulations! Your child is taking the first steps on an exciting journey. The destination? Independent reading!

STEP INTO READING® will help your child get there. The program offers five steps to reading success. Each step includes fun stories and colorful art or photographs. In addition to original fiction and books with favorite characters, there are Step into Reading Non-Fiction Readers, Phonics Readers and Boxed Sets, Sticker Readers, and Comic Readers—a complete literacy program with something to interest every child.

Learning to Read, Step by Step!

Ready to Read   Preschool–Kindergarten
• big type and easy words • rhyme and rhythm • picture clues
For children who know the alphabet and are eager to begin reading.

Reading with Help   Preschool–Grade 1
• basic vocabulary • short sentences • simple stories
For children who recognize familiar words and sound out new words with help.

Reading on Your Own   Grades 1–3
• engaging characters • easy-to-follow plots • popular topics
For children who are ready to read on their own.

Reading Paragraphs   Grades 2–3
• challenging vocabulary • short paragraphs • exciting stories
For newly independent readers who read simple sentences with confidence.

Ready for Chapters   Grades 2–4
• chapters • longer paragraphs • full-color art
For children who want to take the plunge into chapter books but still like colorful pictures.

STEP INTO READING® is designed to give every child a successful reading experience. The grade levels are only guides; children will progress through the steps at their own speed, developing confidence in their reading.

Remember, a lifetime love of reading starts with a single step!

Visit us on the Web!
StepIntoReading.com
randomhousekids.com

Educators and librarians, for a variety of teaching tools, visit us at RHTeachersLibrarians.com

ISBN 978-0-7364-3398-3 (trade) — ISBN 978-0-7364-8215-8 (lib. bdg.)
ISBN 978-0-7364-3399-0 (ebook)

Printed in the United States of America   10 9 8 7 6 5 4 3 2 1

ACROSS THE SEA

By Ruth Homberg

Based on the original story by Brittany Candau

Illustrated by the Disney Storybook Art Team

Random House 🏠 New York

Elsa and Anna are going
on a trip!
They will set sail
to see new places.

Elsa packs.

Anna looks

out the window.

The ship is ready!

Anna steers the ship.
Elsa looks
at the map.

Elsa uses her magic.

She makes a strong wind

to fill the sails.

Land ho!

Soon they arrive

in a new kingdom.

Elsa and Anna meet

the king and queen.

They try new foods.

They see new kinds

of flowers.

The king and queen
throw a party
for Anna and Elsa.

Anna learns
a new dance.

Anna and Elsa
visit another kingdom.
Elsa sees art
with the queen.

Anna plays
with a funny animal!

The queen shows Elsa
a block of ice.
She asks Elsa
to carve
an ice sculpture.

Will Elsa use her magic?

Elsa is too shy.

Anna carves a snowman
in the ice.

It looks like Olaf!

Anna and Elsa
visit another city.
They see the Duke!

The city is very hot.
The Duke does not
like the heat.

Anna and Elsa walk
with the Duke.
Everyone in the city
is hot and sticky.

Elsa wants to help.

She uses her magic.

It starts to snow!

The people cheer!

Elsa makes

frosty drinks.

Everyone feels better.

Even the Duke is happy.

Anna and Elsa

ride sleds.

People ice-skate.

Anna is proud of Elsa.
She sprays the Duke
with snow!
Brrr!

It is time to sail home.

Anna and Elsa wave

goodbye to their

new friends.

They had such a fun trip

across the sea!